W9-AQK-424

DATE DUE

AUG 0 9 1990		
10-7-91		
JUL 14 1998		
NOV 29 '04		
APR 0 2 2012		
JUL 2 0 2012		

j
Fic Gire, Ken
Gir Harmony's hullaba-
     lou at the zoo

STUTSMAN COUNTY LIBRARY
910 5TH ST. S.E.
JAMESTOWN, ND 58401

STUTSMAN COUNTY LIBRARY
BOOKMOBILE
Books for Everyone

DEMCO

J
Fic
Gir

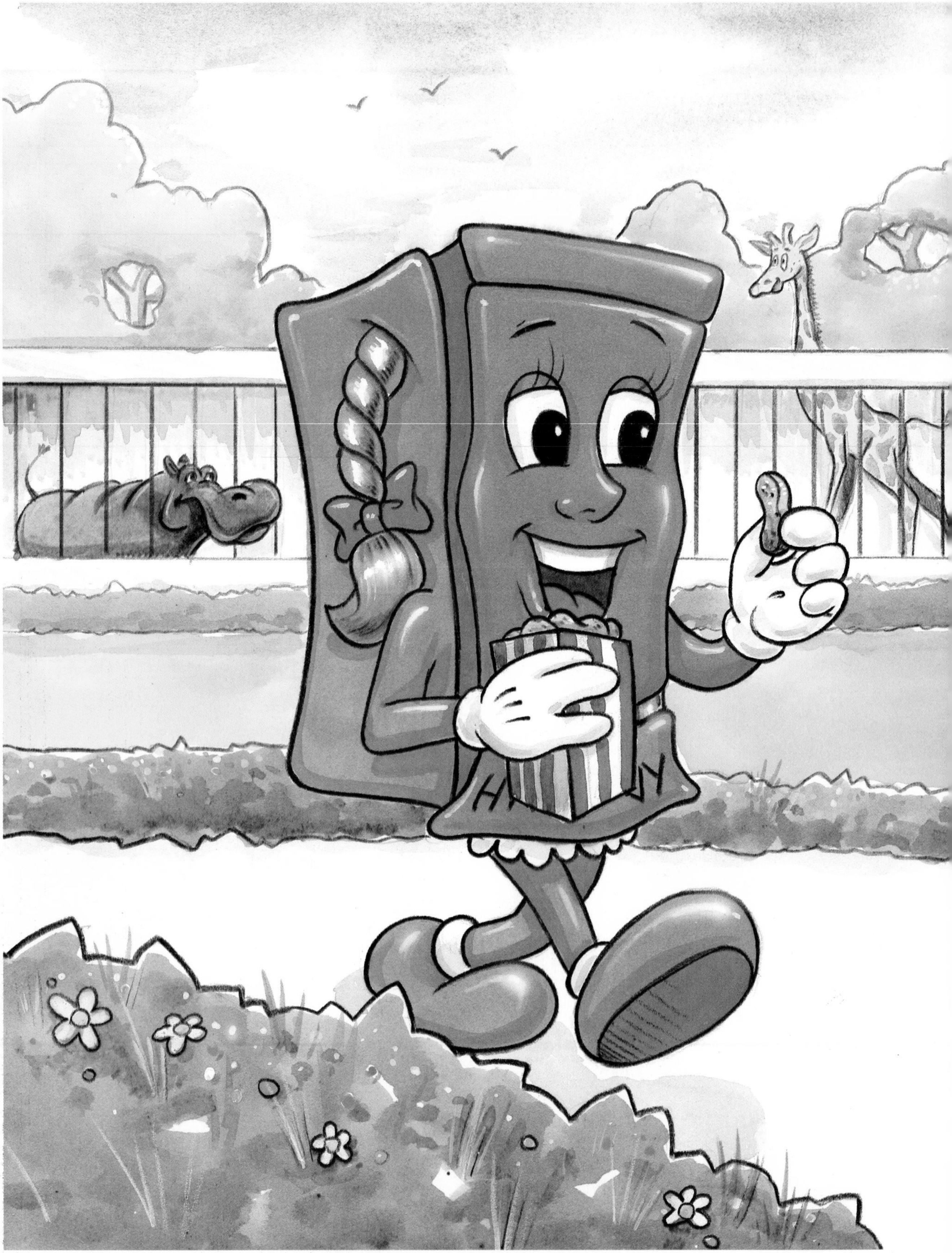

Harmony's Hullabaloo at the Zoo

A Story About Dealing With Fears

Featuring the Psalty family of characters
created by Ernie and Debby Rettino

Written by Ken Gire
Illustrated by John Dickenson,
Matt Mew, and Bob Payne

From Focus on the Family Publishing/Maranatha! for Kids

Pomona, CA 91799. Distributed by Word Books, Waco, Texas.

© Copyright 1988 Focus on the Family Publishing

Psalty family of characters are copyright Ernie Rettino and Debby Rettino, and are administered worldwide by Maranatha! Music as follows: Psalty © 1980; Psaltina © 1982; Melody, Harmony, Rhythm © 1982; Charity Churchmouse © 1984; Provolone, Mozzarella and Limburger (Cheeses for Jesus) © 1984; Churchmouse Choir © 1984; Risky Rat © 1984. These characters are trademarks and service marks of Ernie Rettino and Debby Rettino. Maranatha! for Kids and Kids' Praise are trademarks of Maranatha! Music.

No part of this book may be reproduced or copied without written permission from the publisher.

Library of Congress Catalog Card Number 87-81590
ISBN 084-9999-987

WITHDRAWN
STUTSMAN COUNTY LIBRARY
910 5TH ST. S.E.
JAMESTOWN, ND 58401

"How about a trip to the zoo?" Psalty, the singing songbook, asked his three booklets, Melody, Harmony, and Rhythm.

"We'll see the rhinos, tigers, and camels," their mother Psaltina added, "and even pet some baby animals."

"Hooray! Let's go!" the three booklets cheered, clapping in excitement.

So off the family went.

"We're almost there!" exclaimed Psalty as they neared the iron gates.

"What's your favorite animal, kids?" asked Psaltina.

Harmony answered first: "My favorite is the elephant."

"Mine is the peacock," responded Melody.

"Lion," said Rhythm, forming his hands into claws and growling, "GRRRR!"

Then Psaltina gave the booklets some last-minute instructions: "Don't feed the animals. Don't get too close to the cages. And please, remember to stay together."

As they strolled along, they soon discovered it was a bad day at the zoo. The beavers all had fevers, the gnu got the flu, and the chimpanzees started to sneeze. The weasles had come down with measles, the snakes had the shakes, and even the porcupines had begun to whine.

But just when the booklets were feeling the saddest because the animals were so sick, along came a man pushing a snack cart.

"Cotton candy! Popcorn! Hot roasted peanuts!" he called out.

As the cart passed, all sorts of yummy smells filled the air.

"Can we have some treats, Dad, can we?" the booklets asked, jumping up and down.

"Sounds like a great idea!" Psalty responded.

So Rhythm picked cotton candy, Melody wanted popcorn, and Harmony selected hot roasted peanuts.

Harmony took the bag of steaming peanuts and held them up to her nose.

''Mmmm! They smell s-o-o-o-o good,'' she thought to herself, and then ate the whole bag until only one little peanut was left. Clutching it tightly in her hand, Harmony decided she would save it until she got home.

But without warning, that last little peanut squirted from Harmony's grasp. She stopped to pick it up, but the walkway was long and steep. End over end, the last little peanut just kept rolling . . . and rolling . . . and rolling . . . !

Finally, the peanut reached the bottom of the hill. And right behind it, panting and out of breath, scurried Harmony.

A crowd of people was moving all around her. Looking up the hill for her family, she couldn't see anyone familiar, and Harmony felt just a little bit afraid.

She bent down to grab the last little lost peanut, but all she could see were shoes—sloppy sneakers and skinny sandals and leather loafers and all sorts of clunky clodhoppers. She started to feel more scared—she was so small, and there were so many big shoes. Where *was* that peanut?

Then Harmony saw the peanut through all the legs and feet. She reached between the shoes to pick it up.

But somebody accidentally kicked it.

She reached for it again.

But someone else kicked the peanut, and it scooted out of reach.

Harmony tried to snatch it up again, but—

"Owww!" she hollered as one of the shoes stepped on her fingers.

Harmony felt as small and helpless as that lost little snack. Oh, where were her Mom and Dad?!

Then Harmony glanced down, and right in front of her lay the last luscious little lost peanut.

''There you are!'' she said with joy. ''Found at last! Now if I could find my family . . .''

But just as she started to pick up her lonely last luscious little lost peanut, a pretty peacock pecked the peanut and pranced proudly past Harmony down the pathway, with the snack in its beak.

"Wait!" Harmony called. "Where do you think you're going with my peanut?"

Then she started chasing the peacock. But the faster Harmony ran, the faster the peacock ran.

Finally, Harmony began to gain ground on the bird. She reached out as far as she could and almost grabbed some bright tail feathers. Then the peacock tripped.

As it tumbled into a somersault, the big bird dropped the little peanut.

This launched the lonely last luscious little lost peanut into the air.

It came down on the lawn in front of the elephant's cage. Tiptoeing over to the pen, Harmony hoped that the elephant wouldn't see the peanut—or her!

She no sooner had put the peanut in the palm of her hand than the elephant's long gray trunk snaked its way through the bars and sucked that scrumptious snack right into its snout.

"Give my peanut back!" Harmony demanded, pulling on the elephant's long nose. As she did, the elephant began winding its trunk around her.

She was really scared now!

But fortunately the elephant sneezed, making him uncoil
his snout and sending the peanut flying into the air.

Harmony raced after the peanut, trying to catch it before it
fell to the ground.

But the launched lonely last luscious little lost peanut
landed in the living room of—the lion!

Because Harmony was busy trying to grab the peanut, she ran right between the bars and into the lion's cage. When the lion saw Harmony, he licked his lips, bared his teeth, and roared, "GRRRRRRR!"

Harmony was so frightened she couldn't move. Her scream was even too afraid to come out.

She closed her eyes as the lion came closer . . . and closer . . . and closer!

But faster than you can turn this page—

STUTSMAN COUNTY LIBRARY
910 5TH ST. S.E.
JAMESTOWN. ND 58401

A zookeeper's arm reached through the bars and pulled Harmony to safety.

Harmony cried and cried and cried.

You can imagine how she felt. She was separated from her family, stepped on by a shoe, stolen from by a peacock, squeezed by the snout of an elephant, and now scared by some lion.

''There, there,'' said the woman kindly as she held Harmony. ''You're safe now. Let's go find your parents.''

So the nice zookeeper took Harmony to the main office and made an announcement over the loudspeaker, telling her parents where to find her.

Meanwhile, Psalty, Psaltina, Melody, and Rhythm had been looking high and low, far and near, right and left for Harmony.

When they heard the announcement, they breathed a sigh of relief and rushed over to where she was.

After a round of hugs and kisses, Harmony told them all about her adventure with the lost peanut.

"I'll bet you understand now," said Psaltina, "how dangerous it can be if you wander off by yourself."

"Oh, yes, Mom, I'll never do that ever, ever again—I promise!"

"Were you scared, Harmony, were you?" Rhythm asked excitedly.

"Plenty scared," answered Harmony.

"Sometimes fear can be a good thing," Psalty explained, giving Harmony a reassuring hug. "It can help to make us careful."

"Like when crossing the street," offered Melody.

"Or to keep us away from wild animals!" Harmony exclaimed.

"But even when we're scared," added Psaltina, "we can know that God looks out for us in ways we can't see. He has guardian angels watching over us."

"You mean real angels are watching out for me?" Harmony asked in surprise.

"That's right, sweetheart," said Psalty.

"Sort of like that nice zookeeper?"

Psaltina nodded. "That's why we don't have to be afraid. God and His angels are with us."

"Even in the darkest, scariest moments of our lives," Psalty added, "God is there."

Harmony started to feel all warm inside—and she wasn't scared anymore, knowing how much God, the angels, and her parents were watching over her.

On their way out of the zoo, they passed the man with the snack cart again.

"Cotton candy! Popcorn! Hot roasted peanuts!" he called out.

Harmony looked up at her parents and said, "I think I've had enough hot roasted peanuts for one day!"

"Yes, enough peanuts," said Psalty, with a smile.

"And enough hullabaloo at the zoo," Psaltina added, as they all linked hands and headed for home.